Little Bears go to School

Heather Maisner

Illustrated by
Tomislav Zlatic

W

FRANKLIN WATTS

LONDON•SYDNEY

Evie

Hello. I'm Big Bear. The little bears are going to school and I'm helping out today. Little Evie Bear has come with me but she likes playing hide-and-seek.

School for Little Bears

There's lots of clearing up to do, and
the school pets have gone missing.
Can you help me, please?

Coat

Glove

School bag

Just look at the cloakroom! The little bears have dropped some of their belongings on the floor. Can you point to where they belong?

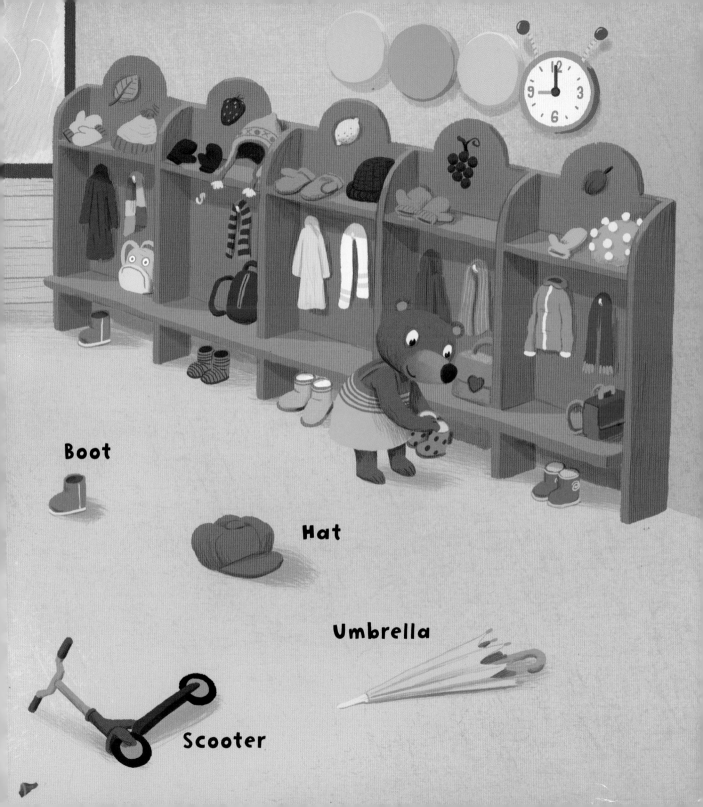

Boot

Hat

Umbrella

Scooter

Thank you. Now where is little Evie Bear?
And did you see something flutter by?

A butterfly flew in while we were busy. Can you see it? And can you see the worm that wriggled in from the garden?

Scissors

Puzzle piece

Pencil

Now we're in the reading and writing corner. What a messy corner it is! Where do all these things belong?

Map

Shape

Ruler

Building block

Book

That's better. Can you find little Evie Bear? I think I saw the school kitten jump in through the window. Can you see her?

And can you find the little blue collar with a bell that she was wearing round her neck?

Doll

Now we're in the home
corner. Just look how many
things there are to put away!

Fancy dress

Pan

Knife and fork

Weights

Milk

Blanket

Teddy

Well done.
Oh no, the
school budgie has escaped
from his cage! And I think I
saw a caterpillar crawling about.

Can you find them both, please?
And where is little Evie Bear?

Jug

Sponge

Fish

We're in the water and sand corner now and things are toppling about all over the place. We really need to put them back neatly.

Bucket

Camel

Plant

Boat

Spade

Things are definitely looking better.
I wonder where Evie Bear is hiding?
And did you hear that clucking sound?

The school chicken is running around and and I think she's laid an egg. Can you find the chicken and her egg, please?

Paper

Apron

Here we are in the painting corner.
It's very untidy. Where do you think
these things should go?

Glue

Paint brush

Paint lid

Crayon

Picture

That's much better. But now the school hamster has escaped from his cage and a snail has crawled in from the playground.

Can you spot them both and can you find Evie Bear?

Hamster

Chicken

All my little bears are having fun in the playground. But now it is time to line up to go home. Please give each little bear the correct hat and scarf.

Dog

Budgie

Kitten

And please put each pet in
the correct place.

Well done!
But a frog and a
duck just leapt out
of the school pond.

Can you spot them both?

Home at last! The school is tidy and all the little bears and the school pets are safely asleep. I do hope you'll come and see us again.

More from the Little Bears!

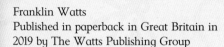

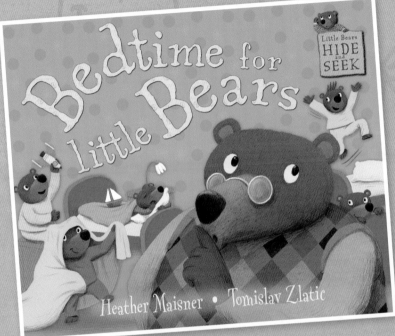

978 1 4451 4323 1

Little Bears go Shopping
978 1 4451 4325 5

Little Bears go on a Picnic
978 1 4451 4329 3

Franklin Watts
Published in paperback in Great Britain in
2019 by The Watts Publishing Group

Text copyright © Heather Maisner 2015
Illustrations © Tomislav Zlatic 2015

The rights of Heather Maisner to be identified as
the author and Tomislav Zlatic to be identified
as the illustrator of this Work have been asserted
in accordance with the Copyright, Designs and
Patents Act, 1988.

Series Editor: Sarah Peutrill
Cover Designer: Cathryn Gilbert
ISBN: 978 1 4451 4327 9

Printed in China

Franklin Watts
An imprint of
Hachette Children's Group
Part of The Watts Publishing Group
Carmelite House
50 Victoria Embankment
London EC4Y 0DZ

An Hachette UK Company
www.hachette.co.uk

www.franklinwatts.co.uk

MIX
Paper from
responsible sources
FSC® C104740
FSC
www.fsc.org